The Foodie Club

The Foodie Club

written by
Dani Shear

illustrated by
Holly Weinstein

Blackbird Books
New York – Los Angeles

Thank you to my two gentle daughters, Sydney, my adventurous eater and Sunny, my mac & cheese girl. You, my swans, are the inspiration for this book. Thanks to my supportive husband, Brian, for listening to many a meter. – D.S.

To my family, Aaron, Aidan, and Julia, for encouraging me to expand my palate . . . and my palette. – H.W.

food·ie

/'fü·dee/

noun, informal

1. a person who is enthusiastic about food; enjoys growing or selecting it, preparing it, and of course, eating it!

I know this young lady named Syd
Who loves to slurp pasta and SQUID
The waiters all gaped

As Syd scraped off her plate

Into her mouth, tentacles slid

Raw fish is her absolute fave

Spicy tuna, Syd does crave

Her friends think it's strange

But Syd will not change

When it comes to NEW food, she's brave

Now Syd has a wee sister, Sunny

Who's picky with food for her tummy

She sure plays it safe

Your typical waif

There isn't much grub she finds yummy

See, Sunny does not have the palate

She won't even venture a shallot

Her mom wants to scream,

"PLEASE BE ON OUR TEAM!

All foodies should love a good salad."

At a picnic they went to last week

They sat by a whispering creek

When the pizza did come

Syd said to her mom,

"I'll have the ANCHOVY and LEEK!"

But Syd's little sis barely ate
The pizza just lay on her plate
"The cheese wants a ride
Down your belly-bound slide,"
Sunny's mother tried hard to bait

Their poor mom could no longer cope

She reached the last knot on her rope

So she hatched a plot

Then ran out and got

A doctor's stethoscope

The next time the girls played PRETEND

A fair princess who's on the mend

A princess who's sick

Needs medicine quick

A "doctor" was summoned to tend

The wise Doc told her she must rest

And to also "please ingest

Pink salmon for strength

For hair to grow length

Cottage cheese makes skin glow its best."

"Seaweed is now found at the store
Not just for MERMAIDS anymore!
There's humus too
A smooth chick-pea stew
With pita, you'll surely adore."

"Try oatmeal, fruit, and a smoothie

A killer breakfast for a foodie

Brown rice and black beans
Keep QUEENS in their jeans
Eat well and you'll never feel moody."

Sunny listened attentively
She so wanted to be healthy
So she PROMISED to try
Food crunchy and dry
And green and nutrient wealthy

So Syd put her sis to the test
To the kitchen she ran on a quest
"I'll blend something sweet
That you're sure to eat
A healthy shake with some ZEST!"

She pulled out the cinnamon sticks

Remembered her mom's little tricks

Almond milk, dates and kale

Honey, bananas (a tad stale)

Went into the big Vitamix

It was time for Sunny to taste
Her big fear, she had to face

So she pinched her nose

And scroonched her toes

And gulped down the shake in a haste

And suddenly, wouldn't you know

A smile, she started to show

Then Sunny let out

The world's *BIGGEST* shout,

And if Miss Sunny dug the drink
Neighbors might also, don't you think?

They drew a big sign:

GREEN SHAKe... it's DiViNe!

They wrote in BOLD black ink

Out the windows their neighbors did peep

The line to taste was five persons deep

Cars screeched to a halt

To try this new malt

For one's health, no price is too steep

The girls were surprised and much pleased
The sisters yelled, "VICTORY SEIZED!"
Despite the big mess
'Twas a huge success
The day had flown by like a breeze

So, dear reader, here comes the rub

Expand your culinary grub

Like Sunny and Syd,

Those adventurous kids,

Start up your own FOODIE CLUB!

I pledge to be a foodie, adventurous and brave

Keep my taste buds curious, no matter what I crave

Try new exciting foods from the East, West, North and South

Keep an open mind, and of course, an open mouth

JOIN THE FOODIE CLUB!

Here's how:

1. Recite "The Foodie Pledge" to a family member.
2. Collect all of the foodie badges.
3. Try out Syd & Sunny's Green Smoothie Recipe.

My Foodie Club Badges

1. Rainbow Meal

2. Tastebud Tester

3. Clean Plate Club

4. Try a Bite

5. Sous-Chef

6. Food Groupie

7. Smoothie Foodie

8. Water Wise

9. Fruit Picker

10.
Global Gourmet

11.
ABC's! Pass the Peas

12.
Go Vegan

Create your own

Create your own

Create your own

How to Earn Badges

Place a sticker of your choosing on a badge after fully completing the requirements.
Ask a grown-up to help.

Eat one meal with different colorful foods. (green beans, red apples, brown rice)

While blindfolded, use those tastebuds, and guess what Mom or Dad offers.

Devour a healthy meal, leaving a shiny, clean plate.

Be polite and try a bite of a new food.

Help Mom or Dad prepare a meal.

Eat a meal with items from each food group.

Invent a new, creative smoothie.

Through the course of one day, drink six glasses of water.

Pick fruit or vegetables with Mom/Dad from a garden or farm to enjoy.

Taste foods from a different culture or country.

Eat three vegetables in alphabetical order. (asparagus, broccoli, carrots)

For one meal, don't eat meat or any foods with animal products.

Syd & Sunny's

Green Shake

A simple smoothie recipe for foodies of all ages:

INGREDIENTS:

1 banana

1 large kale leaf, ripped up

A nice handful of spinach

2 cups of almond milk or rice milk

6 dates with no pits

3 raw walnuts

1 cup of ice

DIRECTIONS:

Blend in a Vitamix or large blender until smooth enough to pour into a tall glass.

Makes one large serving or a few small servings.

** Vary the number of dates according to how sweet you want it.

** Substitute 1 cup of frozen pineapple chunks and 1/2 cup of apples instead of the dates, if you prefer.

Dani Shear lives in Southern California with her daughters Sydney and Sunny, her husband Brian, and her Labradoodle Whisky. When she's not walking Whisky, Dani writes TV pilots as well as humor pieces for various mommy blogs and parenting magazines. This is Dani's first children's book. Dani used to sing all over the country including on Broadway, but now just sings, raps, juggles rubber duckies, acts out parts of Caillou, and performs a one-woman Cirque de Sunny to get her wee one to eat something healthy.

Holly Weinstein despises beans. Lima, black, pinto-you name it. But while illustrating "The Foodie Club," Holly realized she had to set a better example for her own kids; so she tried the loathsome legumes again and again. And guess what? She still doesn't like them, but her son, daughter and husband-who LOVE beans-are proud of her for trying. She has illustrated many books for children and lives in Dallas with her family.

Illustrations rendered in acrylics.

Manufactured in the United States of America.

Cataloging-in-Publication Data
Shear, Dani.
The foodie club / Dani Shear ;
illustrated by Holly Weinstein.
p. cm.
Summary: Two sisters, one an adventurous eater and the other a picky one,
band together to form the "Foodie Club."
1. Food—Juvenile fiction. I. Title.
PZ8.S5437 Fo 2013 [E]—dc22 2013952521

Blackbird Books
www.bbirdbooks.com
email us at editor@bbirdbooks.com

ISBN 978-1-61053-027-9

First Edition
10 9 8 7 6 5 4 3 2 1

CPSIA information can be obtained
at www.ICGtesting.com
Printed in the USA
LVXC02n1223061213
364197LV00012BA/89

* 9 7 8 1 6 1 0 5 3 0 2 7 9 *